FROM THE BEST OF ALL TIME
THE INVISIBLE
DIMENSION
mythical worlds of adventures
ZARA HASSAN
PART I

THE INVISIBLE DIMENSION

Mythical Worlds of Adventure

Part I

Zara Hassan

First off to produce a portal to Kungawo's realm without the necklace was impossible.

And now, oh, good, the kids are fighting again. Nobody said listening to kids bicker is fun. But staying together offers a chance to learn to resolve conflicts, survive and thrive on their own.

Alessa, Mia, Liam and David find themselves thrust into a different dimension where their friendship unfolds with hilarious results. "Hey!" it shouted. David jerked back. "I can groom myself!" the cheetah said.

They love, they hate, and they bicker! But they remain together and must fight the ghost soldiers.

Mia was scared but not because of the mammothian.

An interesting read for the young world, how a group of 4 adventure loving kids solve the mysteries of different dimensions.

A fiction and fantasy for kids ages 7-10 years with amazing story and message for keeping true friends

Genre: Fiction, Fantasy

Age group: 7 to 10

Keywords

#enchanted #magma-rock #fiction #comics #children #humor #middle-grade #friends #adventure #alternate-reality

Contents

CHAPTER 1 – SLEEPOVER INVITATION 5
CHAPTER 2 – A TRIP TO THE WEAPON STORE 10
CHAPTER 3 – THE BEGINNING OF THE ADVENTURE 16
CHAPTER 4 - KIDNAPPED 21
CHAPTER 5 – IN THE CASTLE 28
CHAPTER 6 – RESCUING MIA 34
CHAPTER 7 – TO THE HIDEOUT 40
CHAPTER 8 – TEAM UP AND FIGHT 46
CHAPTER 9 – ARMOR AND FIGHT 56

CHAPTER 1 – SLEEPOVER INVITATION

Lost the necklace

Alessa rummaged through the chest, throwing everything over her shoulder. "Mom! Come here please! I can't find it! My necklace is lost forever!" she howled. Her mom came in the room and shook her head disapprovingly. "I will help you find it but first CLEAN UP YOUR ROOM!" her mom said crossly and went out.

Alessa groaned and muttered "Why do I have to? My necklace is important to use in travels of the invisible dimensions". When she was about to dump her clothes in her closet, her older annoying brother marched in and said "I'm going to the cinema, sis, so don't call me". Alessa rolled her eyes. "Is it like I ever call you?" she shot. "Why so moody?" her brother grinned "Oh, I see. You lost your necklace and messed up your room, eh?", "Go away, Matteo" Alessa said. So he laughed annoyingly and went.

"I have to call Mia, Liam and David" she said quietly. "Are you done cleaning your room?" her mom's voice asked. She saw her mom and nodded. Her mom smiled and pulled out a necklace. "Mom!" Alessa yelled, rushing to hug her mom and snatching the necklace. "Mia called you over for a night, do you want to go?" Her mother asked. "Definitely!" Alessa said, grabbing the telephone.

Ring . . . ring . . . ring . . . "Hello? Alessa, are you coming?" Mia's voice asked in one long breath. "Yeah, are Liam and David coming?" Alessa asked. "Of course" Mia said. After a pause, she said "I heard your necklace got lost. Did you find it?". "Thank god, yes, Mom did" Alessa said "I'm never going to lose it again!" Mia laughed and hung up. That late afternoon, Alessa packed her adventure belongings in her brown rucksack. She put a torch, a rope ladder, a water bottle, her favorite ChocoChippo biscuit, her sleeping bag and diary. She wore her necklace, too. Soon, Mia's mother was waiting outside in her car to pick her. "Wow, you look like you're going to an adventure" she said, smiling. Alessa smiled back and waved goodbye to her mother.

Gang up now

When they reached there, the door burst open and Mia, Liam and David came running out. "You finally came!" David said. "I know" Alessa said "honestly! My necklace got lost". Liam's eyes widened. "Did you find it?" he asked. "Duh, as if I'd come if I didn't" Alessa said, flipping her necklace. "Good, let's eat now" David said. So they all went in and sat on the table, much to Elena, Mia's house helper's, delight. "Little kids, you all were" she said, slipping fresh cabbages and fried chicken on David's plate, who smacked his lips "and now you're all grown! I love cooking food for you twelve year olds, of course".

Moments later, they all ate with quite an appetite. "Oh, Mia. What's the plan next?" Liam asked. Mia stroked her non existing beard. "Hmm, we could sit and talk in the garden, let's go outside in the open air." she suggested. This plan sounded good. Everyone took their rucksacks and sat down in the garden. "I actually want to go to the invisible dimension again!" Alessa said. "I'm fine with that" David said. He loved creepy stuff. "But- but there is ghosts!" Mia protested. "Yes and" David said "that's why we're going there". Mia narrowed her eyes so Alessa spoke before a fight would break. "So are we going?" she asked. "Yes from me" David said at once. "Me too" Liam said. They looked at Mia. She sighed. "I guess I'll come, too" she said finally.

Enchanted rock and magma rock

They all grinned. "Alright, anyone remember the portal that Kungawo gave us?" Liam asked. "I think he gave it to David" Mia said. David opened his mouth indignantly and said "Surely not, he gave it to Mia". Now Mia glared at him and said "What? No! Alessa has it". Alessa held up her necklace and grinned. "I do have it, as a matter of fact" she stated. "Alright" David said hastily "Why don't you open it up?"

So Alessa and the others went to the Enchanted Rock and pointed the necklace's charm diamond on the right spot and the portal appeared, causing a lot of noise and wind blew heavily. "Jump in, everyone!" Alessa yelled, holding on the necklace. Liam, Mia and David jumped in and then Alessa went in with her necklace.

She fell on a hard magma rock on her butt. "Youch!" she cried. "Are you okay?" she saw Mia holding out a hand. Alessa nodded and grabbed her hand. "Okay, so this place gives me shivers" Mia said "but no problem, once we get in touch with Kungawo, we'll be good". Liam nodded confidently. "Let's go to his castle" he ordered. "But does anyone remember the way?" David asked. "Ask the horses, right there, they can talk, remember?" Mia reminded them.

Grooming cheetah

Liam's face lit up and he scurried to a horse, followed by his friends. "Hi, mister horse, do you know the way to Kungawo's castle?" David asked. "Yes, I do, noble visitors, you have to go around the woods, probably half a kilometer, then take a left turn and you'll see Kungawo's castle" the horse replied. They all turned and squinted to see the woods, then turned back to the horse. "I guess we'll get going, thanks, mister horse!" Alessa said and they all walked quickly around the woods.

They stopped by to pat some animals that they found lurking on the border of the woods. "Guys" Mia said suddenly gripping David's arm "is that a cheetah?" she pointed a trembling finger at the little cub. David laughed and pulled his arm. "It's so little!" he said, using one finger to pat its whiskers. "Hey!" it shouted. David jerked back. "I can groom myself!" the cheetah said. "I-I wasn't grooming you" David stammered as the rest of them laughed. "David, are you scared of cheetahs'?" Mia teased. David looked terrified and rushed behind Liam. "C'mon, bro" Liam said, grinning at the cheetah.

Sakura

Still laughing, they reached the castle. "Someone kindly remind me" David said "does anyone live with Kungawo?" Mia shook her head. "No one, except Sakura" she answered "But she's only the helper and there is more than Sakura, also Hiroto and Kenji". "I wonder why he has Japanese helpers" she said thoughtfully. "Maybe because they have interesting personalities" Liam reasoned. "Maybe" David shrugged "But we got to get going". They hurried to the castle and went in. "Hello?"

Mia said loudly. "Kungawo? It's us, Alessa, Mia, David and Liam" Alessa yelled. "Calm down" a familiar voice said behind them.

They all turned and said "Sakura!" She was a tall, fair woman with short, brown, straight hair. "What do you kids want now?" she asked. "We - er – came for a visit in, uh, hopes of dealing with a mission, you see" David said awkwardly. They all nodded. "Alright, you all, follow me and I shall take you all to Kungawo" Sakura said.

They all followed her to a bedroom, Alessa assumed. "Please wait here" Sakura told them. She leaned in the room and said something and pushed the door open for them. They all entered and saw Kungawo smiling and seated on an armchair. "Kungawo! How are you?" Liam said, as they all rushed to him. "I am doing well, I am sure I could survive" he answered, with a serious expression. "What'd you mean?" David asked.

CHAPTER 2 – A TRIP TO THE WEAPON STORE

Long story

"It's a long story" Kungawo said "Do you care to have tea with us and I would tell you?" They all nodded eagerly. "Very well" Kungawo said. Then he turned to Sakura. "Please fetch the tea, will you?" he asked. "Yes, in no time" Sakura said. "So what's the story?" David asked when they settled on the table with the tea in front of them.

"It started" Kungawo began "when you all left from your first visit here, Brantley decided that it was time he struck his addiction to rule The Invisible Dimension again. I, over here, am – or was – powerful enough to stop him and the only one who could. It was, until, he cursed me and now I cannot stop him and his evil work" he went on "and he knew that you children are, well, just children so he put something in you all that made you come here. Before I could send Tiffany to warn you not to come, but you did." He said.

"We're glad we came" Alessa said "we could help you!" "What is Brantley doing?" David asked. "He is pushing out his Ghost Soldiers –

I'm sure you remember them – to fight and kill everyone so the only thing in the world would be left is the Ghost Soldiers, and that" Kungawo said "is insane". They all understood but Liam raised a question. "What are you cursed for?" he asked Kungawo. "I am not able to use my powers anymore" Kungawo answered. "Hmm" Mia said "maybe we could stop him". Kungawo's eyes widened and Sakura breathed "Oh no! It is too dangerous!" David nodded. "Yes, it is and the only way to stop danger is to pass danger" he found himself saying. "Wise words!" Kungawo exclaimed "Very smart boy!"

David went red and grinned. "Of course" he said. Mia rolled her eyes and laughed. "I don't think he even knew what he was saying" she giggled. "Well, Miss Very-Smart Mia suggested it" David said, grinning. Mia smiled grimly. "How do we start?" Alessa asked. "I guess go to Brantley's place" Liam said. "I will get a plan ready by morning" Kungawo said "you must sleep now".

Lost the necklace

Sakura led them to the rooms and they snored till she knocked on their doors next morning. "Wake up!" she called. "Coming" David's sleepy voice came. They were in for the breakfast just in time. "Good morning" Kenji greeted them. "G'morning, Kenji" Alessa said, as the others smiled. "What's the plan?" David asked when they sat on the breakfast table. "Well" Kungawo said "we can go to the weapon store and get some weapons from there and then we could attack Brantley in his castle". Mia frowned. "Attack? But . . . "she protested. "It is the only option, unless you want Brantley to attack first" Kungawo said firmly.

"C'mon, Mia" Liam said "We'll be good. We can't let him scare us, can we?" Mia's lips made a straight line. "I don't know . . . I guess not" she shrugged. David rolled his eyes. "Look, Mia can stay here if she's freaking out, but we're going" he said. Mia glared at him. "Look who's talking" she mumbled. Kungawo turned to Mia. "Do you think you can go? I know it is dangerous, but it's to save the dimension, unless you don't *want to* help" he said stiffly. The others looked at her. Mia took a deep breath and said "We'll do it! Let's go to the weapon store". Alessa grinned and hugged Mia. Kungawo smiled gratefully. "Thank you, you kids, very nice and smart" he complimented.

They all soon arrived in the Weapon Store. They looked around. It had bright blue walls and weapons firmly strapped on the walls with dark brown belts. Gray tables were spread in rows of six. "This place is Humungous" Liam said. They all nodded in agreement. "Welcome to the Weapon Store" a quick raspy but squeaky voice said, a few feet further than them. They all peered and saw a white, wooly, with two small brown horns on the head, sheep. "A sheep?" David asked, trying not to laugh. The sheep smiled sweetly. "What are all your names?" she asked.

"Alessa" Alessa said. "I'm Liam" Liam said. "David and that's Mia" David said. Mia said "I could introduce myself without help, *David*". David shrugged. "Was just helping" he said, grinning. "My name is Kungawo" Kungawo said. The sheep did a small smile. "Oh! Noble Kungawo, I know you!" she exclaimed. "Well, how do you do?" Alessa asked the sheep after a pause. The sheep sighed. "I do this and I do that and this and that and this and that", she said.

Disintegrate 'em all

David raised his eyebrows. "That's, uh, quite normal, not weird at all or anything", he said. The sheep turned jerkily to him. He took a step back. "Young man, come closer and I will tell you something" the sheep said. David slowly and hesitantly came close to the sheep and the sheep whispered "My name is Sheepie". He pulled himself back awkwardly. "Oh, ok" he said. Then he turned and looked at the others and caught them trying not to laugh. "Young man, huh?" Mia said, giggling. David reddened and said to Sheepie "And I am not a young man, just a boy of twelve years old". Sheepie nodded. "Yes, yes, twelve years" She said.

They shrugged at the weird sheep and continued to look around. "What is it that you fellows want now?" she asked. "Well, we're in the Weapon shop, so we'd obviously want weapons, right?" Mia said. "Ah, weapons. They are very important nowadays especially since, well, Brantley started invading. But the Ghost Soldiers were very mean and stole all the swords available" Sheepie said sadly. Alessa felt a little sorry for her so she said "It's OK, I'm sure we can find other weapons . . .", Sheepie smiled, but the look of sadness stayed in her eyes. *She probably loves her store a lot,* Alessa thought.

"What about a gun?" Liam said suddenly. "What about it?" David said. "Disintegrator gun!" Liam answered, trying to pull out a small pistol out of the strap. "It ain't going to work if you pull it" the sheep said. "Then you try" Liam said, backing off so that Sheepie had space to remove it. She went over and gently pulled the straps end and it opened. She took out the pistol and gave it to Liam. "Oooh" he examined it.

Soon, they all got disintegrators and before they could leave the store, the sheep said "Can I come with you? It'd be delightful if I could, or imagine when I would!" They agreed to bring her, except David who muttered "Why do we need a sheep which can only talk and act weird and possibly pull out disintegrator guns?" Alessa, who heard him, said "Because we need a lot of help, after all, don't we?" David gritted his teeth and nodded slightly.

"Sheepie? Do you want to come with us to my castle?" Kungawo asked. The sheep nodded happily and jumped around. "Oh, yay!" she exclaimed "Me at Noble Kungawo's castle! How exciting! Brilliant! You will be proud to hear that I actually saved a leaf from touching the ground and getting hurt-". "That's a sort of easy thing to do . . ." Liam said. The sheep looked faintly offended. "It's not an easy job; you know" she scoffed "being a sheep doesn't make life easy. Being human is a total different thing! Powerful, important and all good, sheep is only for wool and meat . . ." Alessa stopped listening after a moment. Sheepie talked quite a lot. "Anyway" she said "Let's just get going, you know". So they did.

Sheepie with a teacup

They went back to Kungawo's castle. Sakura opened the door and the door to let them in. "Who's that?" she asked, watching suspiciously to Sheepie. "I am Sheepie, pleased to see you!" Sheepie said brightly. Sakura nodded and said "Well hello, I am Miss Sakura. Sir Kungawo, the living room is ready for the guests". "Yes, I'm coming in a minute, thank you" said Kungawo.

All of them left the main entrance of the castle and were scurrying to the living room. "Welcome, Sheepie" Kungawo said.

Sheepie beamed and took a seat. It was quite odd looking to see a sheep seated on a red velvet armchair, holding a teacup, but that's what Sheepie was doing. "I love this place" Sheepie said, stroking her wooly beard. "Me too" Alessa said, not only because she liked the place, but also because she didn't want an awkward silence to start off and offend Sheepie. "Yep" David agreed, taking a long slurp of his tea. "When should we put our plan in action, Kungawo?" Liam asked. "Right before Lunch time, Liam" Kungawo said. "But we won't be able eat lunch!" Mia said in horror.

"Since when" David said "is the rule of fighting with a full stomach permissible?" Mia grumbled and clutched her teacup tightly. "What's up?" Alessa asked. "I. DON'T. WANT. TO. FIGHT!" Mia screamed. Everyone looked startled. "Calm down, Master Screamer" David told her at last. "Mia, you do not have to fight if you do not want to" Kungawo said calmly. "I do, I do, but it's just . . . "Mia said. "I don't know . . . cowardice?"

Alessa shook her head. "No, you are not a coward, you know that" she said firmly. "She's right" Liam piped up "Your just finding an excuse, don't do that! We need a *brave* Mia". Mia turned red and said "I'll try". David snorted. "If I recall right, that's exactly what you said previously" he said. Mia went redder and said "I'll be good, come *on*". Alessa smiled, breaking the fight. "Good, stop teasing her, David" she ordered. David rolled his eyes, but Alessa made it clear to him that the argument is over. She knew that Mia was scared, but she also knew when Mia puts a plan firmly in her mind once, it doesn't change.

CHAPTER 3 – THE BEGINNING OF THE ADVENTURE

Too hot

"So what now?" Liam asked. "We have some more tea" Kungawo said, pouring the steaming tea from the bright pink teapot into his cup. "Great" Alessa said, pleased for some more of the delicious drink. She drank it too fast when it was still burning hot, and she felt her tongue go numb with burn. She let out a yell. "Ooh!" she cried. They all looked at her and Kungawo smiled cleverly. "Well, it is not every day we learn to blow our tea before drinking it" he said.

Feeling very embarrassed, she grinned and shook her head. Then the children understood. "She burnt her tongue!" Mia exclaimed. "Oh no, very disastrous at that" the sheep said. "We're joking, Sheepie, it's not a real burn" David said, roaring with laughter. The sheep looked puzzled and then she giggled.

"Back to business" Liam said who seemed to be interested in Brantley and wanted to fight him. "Alright" David said. "What 'alright'?" Mia said "We already know; we're leaving before lunch, so that's that". They all looked at her in surprise. "Wow, Mia" Liam said "It's like a *double* brave Mia". Mia grinned and said "I knew it".

So before lunch was when they left. "I wish I could come with you, but I am powerless" Kungawo said sadly. "Don't worry, Kungawo, we'll make sure Brantley returns your powers" Alessa said. "Yeah, and if he doesn't, we will, or we'll *make* him" said David. Mia grinned and said "Whatever happens, remember, Brantley is The Bad Guy, and he will remain like that, so it is, we'll win". Liam nodded. "Great spirit! Let's go!" he yelled as the horses galloped towards the sun.

"I'm a little scared of horses" Mia began. "Not *now*, Mia" Liam cut her off. "I might actually fall off" she reasoned. "Well, then that's good for you" David said. Alessa grimly told them "Can we shut up? Its irritating that you both keep bickering!"

A little too late

So Mia and David kept quiet for the rest of the ride, which Alessa and Liam were thankful for. They reached the castle after what seemed like hours to Alessa. "I actually regret coming here . . ." Mia said, accidently out loud. Her friends jaws went square and the rolled their eyes. "Too late for that, Mia" David said, his blue eyes shining. He got down from his horse and looked at Brantley's hideout with was about twenty meters away.

They walked to the tower and found the gates obviously closed. "Should we – like, go inside in the daylight?" Mia asked. "It's already getting dark" Alessa said. "Oww!" David yelled suddenly. They saw a crab that had clipped on his feet. "Where did *that* come from?" Liam asked distractedly. "I don't know but I'm not going to let it go!" David said. He went up to the crab and gave it a harsh shove.

"Use manners, you claw monster!" he shouted fiercely. "It won't understand you" Mia said. He turned sharply, but didn't say anything and didn't meet her eyes. "Whatever" he mumbled. "At least they didn't argue" Liam whispered to Alessa. She nodded and whispered back "Let's hope this lasts till we attack Brantley". "Did you forget that I am here?" the sheep waved her hand in the air.

"Oh yeah" Liam said. "Do you think it's a good idea if Sheepie stays here?" David asked. Alessa shrugged. "Not sure . . . "Mia murmured. "I guess so" Liam said. "We have to get to Brantley's castle, and some of us can stay here and search his tower and the rest of us can go to the castle" He said. "But what if Sheepie'll be in danger? We can't leave a helpless sheep by herself!" David said.

"*Excuse me? I am not a helpless sheep*" Sheepie huffed "I am better off without you folks, keep underestimating me". With that she turned and went away. Liam glared at David. "You did it! Good job" he said sarcastically. "My pleasure" David said, rolling his eyes. "Stop! Stop fighting!" Alessa cried. "You don't tell me what to do" David said. Alessa was all for starting to cry with frustration, but she pulled herself together and said "Ok, listen to…". "Me" Liam interrupted, smiling at Alessa to let her know that he'd deal with David "We're a team, not arguers, right?" Mia smiled encouragingly. "We are a team" she said. Unexpected to that, David said quietly "Yes". "A team doesn't fight with each other; they fight *for* each other" Liam explained "so we'll wait till the gates open – ".

Give her back!

"As in never? What if it doesn't?" David asked. "Then we'll find out a passage, because there's *got* – 'Liam said, when Mia shrieked. Their heads turned in a split a second. They were just in time to see her getting dragged by the ghost soldiers. "Give her back!" Alessa screamed, running after them. Liam and David followed her. But the Ghost Soldiers were gone.

"Noooo! Why did that just happen?" David yelled. "Come back! Mia!" Alessa wailed. "We can't stand here and scream" Liam said in a shaky voice. Alessa half sobbed "Sh-she's g-g-gone! Ho-how can we not sc-sc-scream?" Liam went to his sobbing friend and said "It's ok; we'll rescue her, Alessa". Alessa looked up and then glanced at David. He was standing there, frozen with horror at what had just happened. "Your right" she said finally. "I know I am" Liam smiled at her. "Let's follow the flying truck!" he pointed at the Ghost Soldier's flying truck.

For the first time, Alessa was grateful that her mom sent her to the strength building gym otherwise she would be lagging behind the boys. The leaped on the shops rooftops and ran quietly in the silent evening. "Hurry" Liam said in a low voice. They obeyed and rushed behind him, avoiding the electricity wires. Alessa tightened her sneakers and balanced herself on the rope and quickly made it to the next building.

"Took you long enough" Liam said. Alessa grinned. "I don't care- hey where's Dave?" she said. They looked around and saw his figure way in the front, creating a silhouetted form David. "Even though they argue a lot, they remind me of Tom and Jerry a bit" Liam whispered, loud enough to be heard by Alessa who nodded.

They catch up to David. "The truck's getting away!" he yelled over the wind's breezy racket. "Let's take a jet or something!" Liam suggested stupidly. "Yes, but how are we going to ride it?" Alessa argued "we're just kids!"

"Maybe it's not a good idea to ride jets . . ." Liam admitted. "Yes, but we have to rescue Mia, right?" David said. "That's right" Alessa said. "I don't know what to do" Liam replied. "I know!" David said. "What?" Alessa and Liam asked at once.

"Since we can't drive the jets, maybe we can *ask* someone to" David went on. "Who are you suggesting, I'd like to know?" Liam asked. "Well, it could be anyone" David replied. "Including the Ghosts soldiers?" Alessa asked in horror. "'Course not" David replied "We could do only one thing . . ."

CHAPTER 4 - KIDNAPPED

Ghost soldiers

Back with Mia, she was tied with spooky Ghost Soldiers. She tried to kick them but, of course, she was tied. "Where are you taking me, you fools?" she yelled. "Shut it, kid" one of them barked rudely. "Oh, not very likely I'd follow your rules" Mia growled. "Well, we'll make you, then!" another Guard said. She tried to punch their jaws, but she couldn't reach them.

Mia grimly looked out of the window and saw her friend's figures running opposite to where she was. "Guys!" she said, knowing that they wouldn't and couldn't hear her. After hours, the truck landed, and she knew that they definitely weren't in Kungawo's castle. "Where are we?" she asked sharply to the Ghost Guards. They didn't answer; instead shoved her out of the truck and an evil looking man came and smiled horribly.

He was wearing a red waist coat and black trousers. He had stringy black hair and an eye patch. "Come here, you girl!" he bellowed. Mia came to him. "You're Mia, aren't you?" he asked, smirking. She nodded, not bothering to answer him. "So that's it" the man said "we're keeping you here, and we'll make your friends work for us or else . . . they'll get to attend your funeral" he laughed evilly.

This statement did not scare Mia. She narrowed her eyes and said "They will *not*". The man chuckled and said "Oh, they will, if they disagree". Mia sighed and felt sorry for her friends, though not as much as she felt for herself. "Alright, I'm coming with you freaks" she announced. "Oh, you are no doubt" said the man. So she was dragged in the huge, black castle with tall dark towers on each side. She suddenly felt very frightened of it and wanted to run away from the man.

Instead, she tried to cope with the bad man and followed him without making a fuss. She tried not to gag at his smelly coat. "C'mon, kid, Sir Brantley probably wants to see your annoyingly idiotic face" the man said, meanly. "How nice of you . . ." Mia muttered angrily. "I heard you" the man said grimly. "I meant you to" Mia spat. "Shut up now, we're going inside, so make a good impression on Sir Brantley" the man said. "I would if he can handle me punching him" mumbled Mia. They very soon were in the gloomy looking hall with one long table in the middle of the room.

Sit down Mia

The man pushed Mia on a couch. "Sit here quietly" he ordered in a low voice. So she sat and waited for what would happen next. Then man motioned her to stay seated and went out. She thought what her friends would be doing. Hopefully planning to rescue her and hopefully Brantley would get hit on his head or something so he won't remember that he is supposed to be a bad guy.

Deep in her thoughts, she gazed around blankly. All of a sudden, the door burst open and in came Brantley. She looked at him, extremely startled at a sudden entrance. "Oh, no, this isn't going to be fun . . ." she mumbled nervously. Brantley looked over at her and smirked.

"Come here, Mia" he demanded her. She didn't move. "No" Mia said quietly. "I said . . . COME HERE!" Brantley roared. She slowly got up and walked to him. Her head started pounding and she began to feel sweaty, yet cold. "Yes?" she asked, still quietly. "You are going to work with me, young lady" he answered. Mia was terrified but she bravely shook her head. "Then, die" Brantley said, in an exasperated tone.

"That's what I'd rather do, you know" Mia said. But then she hesitated. She wasn't sure to die in front of Brantley's satisfied eyes or anywhere *but* this horrid place. "I guess not" she muttered, audibly. "I knew it" Brantley said, smiling cleverly. "So go to sleep" he ordered. The man who Mia had met earlier hurriedly came and said quickly "Yes, sir" and pushed Mia to her room.

As soon as she entered, she felt cold and shivery. She looked around and it took her a while to realize that there was no fire place. She wished that she had some telephone to text her friends and then she remembered. "My disintegrator pistol!" she gasped, pulling it out. She narrowed her eyes and planned her escape.

Young man

Amazement and confusion

Meanwhile, back with Alessa, Liam and David, they hurried back to Kungawo's castle. Sakura opened the door and was shocked to see them back so early. "Oh! How are you back so fast?" she asked. "Mia's kidnapped" David panted "and – ". "*Kidnapped?*" Sakura shrieked. "Yes and" Liam grunted "we came back the ghost soldiers did it. Their flying truck! Brantley probably sent them, you know!" Sakura stared at them in amazement and confusion.

"You guys better come in and start with the story again. I didn't understand a word you said" she claimed. They were brought inside, much to Kungawo's surprise. "What – where is Mia?" asked Kungawo. "She's gotten kidnapped! The ghost soldiers and their flying truck came and took her away!" Alessa cried.

"What?" Kungawo asked. Few explanations later, he understood. "Well, he took her for a reason, and we need to know why" Liam said. "Of course we know why" Kungawo snorted "he'll be sure to make a stupid deal or he'll keep Mia!" The children were horrified. "We *have to* get Mia back" Alessa said finally. "That's right" Liam agreed. So did David.

"We need someone's help, Kungawo!" said David. "Yes, but I recall telling you that I would not be able to help you. You see?" Kungawo answered. "We do, but don't you know *anyone?*" Alessa asked desperately. "No, not many" Kungawo replied "and my assistants would love to help you, but they do not have weapon of any kind, unless a rifle would count, which it would not".

There was a pause. Uncomfortable silence was in the air and everyone could feel that something terrible was going to happen. "Well, guys" Liam said. "Well?" David asked, looking at him. "We can only go to Brantley's castle because it's the biggest problem we have right now, then we have other ones, like Mia kidnapped, or Sheepie left us or something like that" answered Liam.

Good bye

David straightened his back uncomfortably, knowing the reason that Sheepie *had* left them. "Alright, you all can get jetpacks and use them as a transport" said Kungawo. "OK, let's go then" Alessa announced, getting up. They headed to the door and waved goodbye to Kungawo and Sakura.

"Are you scared?" David asked Liam and Alessa. "Yes, but I'll do anything to get Mia back and stop this evil Brantley" Alessa said firmly. "Me too" Liam informed them. "Good, I feel exactly the same" David said. They had left their horses in Brantley's hideout, so they didn't have a transport. They ran instead of using a horse, though they did consider taking a cab, but no cabs existed in the Invisible Dimension.

"Are we nearly there?" Alessa panted. "Not nearly, but not far either" Liam replied "And no sign of the flying Ghost Truck!" David looked around and exclaimed "The Jet Shop!" They stopped. "But" Alessa protested "we need *jetpacks* not jets".

Liam thought for a while and then said "We can do with it, though". "But, Liam! We're only kids, I told you before, we – "Alessa said shocked. "Can't ride jets, I know" Liam interrupted her. Then he squinted at the shop. "Well, that can't be helped. Let's go" he gestured them to follow him.

They entered the dusty and smelly shop. They could smell rusty metal and taste the dirt in the air. "Yuck" David commented. "Look" Alessa pointed at something –

A thing - they could call it- was sitting on a stool. It had claws like a bird and wings like a bird. Yet it was nothing like a bird. It was seven feet tall and seven feet wide. It had antennas poking out of its head and was quite furry. The face had whiskers and looked like a cat. The children stared at it curiously. "What are you?" David asked it. The creature peered at them and that's when they noticed that he was wearing big round thing spectacles.

The Mammothian

"I am a Mammothian" the creature bellowed. Alessa gasped. "Isn't mammoth meaning huge?" she asked. "Yes" Liam said. "Well" the Mammothian said in its deep voice. "We're here for - er – a jet" David stammered. "Yes, jet, I'll fetch 'em" the Mammothian said, getting up and bending his head because the wooden roof was low.

"Have you got a name?" David called as the Mammothian stormed back. The Mammothian blinked. "A what? What's a name?" he asked, because it was clear that it was a 'he' by now. "This guy needs education" Liam muttered to Alessa as David explained the Mammothian "It's your own thing, you know? Like I want to call you Scaley, for instance, and that's your name! Get it?" he said loudly.

"No, I haven't gotten a name, have you got 'em? Have you gotten a name?" the Mammothian asked. "Yes! I am David, that's my name!" David shouted because the Mammothian didn't have good hearing. "Yes, and I'm Alessa! That's Liam, we're friends!" Alessa yelled "do you want to be our friend?"

"I ain't got a friend" the Mammothian said "I ain't known what a friend is. What's a friend?" David sighed. "Never mind" Liam called. "Can I follow? Mister Brantley is mean!" the Mammothian bellowed. "Sure" Alessa said before any of the boys could argue. The Mammothian leaped up and roared "I AM COMING! THE MAMMOTHIAN IS COMING!" This was enough to make the children stumble backwards. "Please don't shout!" Liam roared back.

After a short while, they were all in the jet. "How to drive this?" the Mammothian asked. "You should know! You're the shop keeper!" Liam yelled. "Alright, let's figure this out" David said. A few tries later, they got the hang of it and it glided swiftly off the ground.

"We haven't got much time!" Alessa informed them "We'd better hurry!"

CHAPTER 5 – IN THE CASTLE

Shorty girl and the hunched back

Back in Brantley's castle, when morning had arrived, the bold man had shaken Mia to wake up. When she woke up, she remembered her escape plan. But it didn't go how she expected it to. "C'mon slowpoke" The man said gruffly. She got up sleepily as the man pushed her in the washroom and told her to wash her face.

Few minutes later, the man dragged her to the hall where they went earlier. She shivered as she saw Brantley enter, smiling coldly. "Good morning, sir" the man greeted Brantley hurriedly. Brantley glanced at him dismissively and moved on till he reached Mia. "You!" he said "Ah, I nearly forgot she was here! It is almost time!" Mia wondered time for what. "What?" she asked quietly. "Oh, you'll not want to know, would you?" he asked Mia. She didn't reply to him.

"Well!" Brantley said. Then a hunchbacked man hurried to him and said in a flat voice "Breakfast's ready, sir". Brantley nodded. "I'm coming, and get this shorty girl and stuff some plums in her mouth, that's all she'll get for breakfast" he said, cackling. The hunchback quickly grabbed Mia and pulled her along with him. "You must scream" the hunchback hissed in her ear. "For what?" she asked softly. "Sir Brantley should think I'm tough, so scream! Get on with it" he explained. "Oh no, I won't" Mia said. Then she loudly began to say "How weak you are! You can't even pull me!" Brantley turned with a frustrated look on his face.

"Take her! Do it roughly, go on!" he shouted at the frightened and furious hunchback. The hunchback nodded quickly and tried to pull her harder.

They entered the living room, where Mia supposed that they had their meals there. "Sit!" the hunchback barked. So she sat. After the unpleasant meal, she was taken to a room and she found herself standing in front of Brantley. Suddenly, a few guards came and sort of seized her in a way that she gasped and was suddenly on alert. "Make her shut her mouth" Brantley ordered. They put a hand over her moth that she could barely breathe and then it happened. Brantley transformed into a bat and bit her. She was in the trance now.

Bad Brantley

While this was happening, David was giving a few English lessons to the Mammothian in the jet, while Liam drove it and Alessa pulled out her binoculars. "Oh, look! We're nearly there!" she exclaimed, looking in it. "Really?" Liam asked, glancing over his shoulder. It was late morning already, around eleven.

"Really" Alessa answered, gazing through her binoculars. " . . . And that is how you make a name" David finished telling the Mammothian. "Ohh" he said "What's my name, though? I haven't got one!" David thought for a second. "Your name can be . . . Bear?" he asked. "No!" Alessa shrieked at once. "Hmm . . . then maybe . . . Scaley? Like I suggested in the beginning?" David suggested.

So it was settled. The Mammothian was herby named Scaley. "Scaley, we need your help" Liam said "But – but, your dumb, and you don't know anything. And that doesn't matter, because all you need to know is who Brantley is and how to fight". Alessa glanced at Scaley. "Do you know who Brantley is?" she asked him. He nodded fiercely. "Bad Brantley!" he roared.

"And do you know how to fight?" David asked. "I'll show ya!" Scaley yelled. He was about to crash a hole in the jet when Liam stopped him. "Good, you can show us your talents when we reach down" he said as David and Alessa sighed in relief. Scaley was just like a pet who could talk.

They landed as swiftly as they had glided off before and got out of the jets and stood staring at the castle. "Shall we go in?" Alessa asked. "Well, we didn't come here to start howling and crying to go back home, did we? Of course we go in" Liam said, his voice somewhat sterner. So they all went and knocked on the castle door. "It's not as if we'd get anyone to open the door" David sighed. "Should Scaley break 'em? Should he break the door?" Scaley asked.

They glanced at Liam. "Yes" he nodded "Alright go on". So they got the door broken in no time, but there was a problem –

Not big enough

"There's a passcode door" David groaned "Can you break it, Scaley?" Scaley punched the door and shook his head. "It is too hard".

They tried to think what to do but didn't have any ideas. "OK" Liam said "We'll just have to find a passage or something, I mean, if people enter quite frequently, there wouldn't be a passcode door, and a passageway they all know probably is there" he continued "So all we have to do is to find a passage".

"And pass it" Alessa added "all good". "So where do we start from?" David asked, examining around. "I'm thinking" Liam said. Then "Maybe, from an underground tunnel?" After a moment of thought, they all agreed. This sounded likely and castles usually had dungeons so possibly.

"Are we supposed to find dungeons?" Scaley asked. "Or any other tunnel, burrow or hole" said Liam. "Oh, alright" Scaley said and began searching around for any of the things that Liam had mentioned. "Oh, guys!" Liam called "I might've found the entrance!" They hurried to him. There was a hole, big enough to fit a large dog but not as big for a Mammothian. "It's big, but not big for big creatures" David said, glancing at Scaley. "Does Scaley have to stay behind?" Scaley asked. Liam nodded solemnly. "Perhaps you might have to because, you know, the hole is a little small for you . . ." he said, biting his lips.

"Scaley doesn't want to stay behind but he has to, so he will!" Scaley bellowed "Good luck!" Alessa smiled at Scaley and waved her hand to say goodbye. They slipped inside the hole and made their way in. It was smelly – smelly in the sense, they could smell danger – and cold. "Let's be quiet" Liam advised. So they were. They silently made their way. It was definitely hours since they went in the tunnel. "What time is it?" Alessa whispered to David as he checked his watch. "Around three in the afternoon" he whispered back.

Suddenly, Liam came to a halt. "What is it?" David whispered loudly to Liam. "Didn't you – the sound – "Liam stammered. Alessa and David both listened hard. They didn't hear anything at first, but then the sound of clinking was getting closer. "I hear it" Alessa gasped. Everyone held their breaths, expecting to see a man holding Mia, or Mia coming by herself. What they didn't expect was to see a rabbit. And that's what they saw. "How's this little thing making the racket?" David asked. "It's got a bell around its neck!" Liam pointed out. They touched the bell softly and continued walking without making noise.

No hugging please

Then Liam, who was in the lead, gave a gasp of surprise. "It's a door! Should I – should I open it?" he asked. David and Alessa nodded. So after a deep breath, he clicked it open and they heard a bold voice echoing. "Now punch!" it said and someone's punching sound was made.

Liam peered up and his eyes widened and he pulled Alessa and David up to see what he saw. There was a tall man, standing next to a punching bag and a girl was standing in front of him. "Mia!" Alessa gasped in surprise. David clenched his fist and climbed out before Liam or Alessa could stop him. He stood confidently and said "Mia! Are you OK?" the man and Mia stared at him blankly.

Then the man laughed. Alessa and Liam climbed out after David. "Mia!" Alessa yelled, running to hug her. But when she did, Mia pushed her away roughly. "Ugh, why are you hugging me, you doll face?" she said in a disgusted tone. Alessa, who had stumbled back, caught her balance and squinted at Mia.

"What's wrong with you?" Alessa shrieked *"you know I hate dolls!"* David stepped forward and told Mia "Hello? Do you remember me, David and us all, we're your crew?" Mia wrinkled her nose in disgust and said "More like shoes". "You brainwashed her!" Liam glared at the man, who chuckled. Alessa put her hand on her disintegrator. "Why did you do this?" she asked trying not to yell with anger. Before the man could reply, the door burst open.

CHAPTER 6 – RESCUING MIA

Very clever

In walked Brantley, letting the children shiver at the look of his cold and thin smile. "Well, well, well, *hello"* he said pleasantly. Liam gritted his teeth as Mia bowed to Brantley. "These strangers came from nowhere, My Lord and Master" Mia said respectfully. David's eyes widened. "So she's your little puppet now, as if you didn't have enough, which you didn't" he growled at Brantley. Brantley patted Mia's head and turned to the other three.

"You found our passage, now, didn't you?" Brantley said, not bothering to reply to David. "We did" replied Alessa, narrowing her eyes. "Very clever" Brantley ranted "but not clever enough to know that what may await you at the very end of the passage. Wanted to get in trouble, didn't you?". "That's nothing for *you* to know. Why did you brainwash Mia?" Liam asked, leaping in front of Brantley. Mia stepped forward and nearly punched him on his jaw when Alessa yanked him back.

"Careful!" she hissed. "Yeah" Liam replied. "Don't touch Lord and Master Brantley" Mia roared. "You definitely brainwashed her!" David said, waving a hand in front of Mia's face, who grabbed it and twisted it. David yanked his hand back and nursed it. "Ouch!" he began to shake his hand. "She's become powerful after being under Brantley's control" Alessa noticed. "That's probably because she allowed me to" Brantley said.

"In what condition can you give our friend back to us?" Liam asked sharply. "Well, you must not help the annoying Kungawo – "Brantley started but David growled "How dare yo-". "Let him finish, Dave" Alessa said, pulling him in case he punched Brantley. "I repeat, do not help Kungawo and work for me instead – "Brantley continued. "*Never!*" David bellowed. "Shut up!" Brantley snapped. "You" David said, holding up a finger "don't give *me* orders, get it?" "Oh, quiet down, David" Liam said exasperated. David did not want to calm down, but he grunted and stepped back.

"As I was saying" Brantley began to continue "Don't help Kungawo and work for me or I'll not give Mia back". "We can do the first one, just give her back and un – brainwash her!" Liam blurted. "Alright, good" Brantley said. Then he turned to the man and said something to him in a low voice and both of them exited the room. "Well, Mia?" Alessa asked her. "What?" Mia replied sharply.

Definitely alive

"Don't be his puppet!" David said, charging forward to punch Mia. Liam grabbed him and pushed him back. "Don't do the drama right now" He said sternly to David. "But, Liam! She's brainwashed so just a tiny knock on her head would get her back to normal – whoa, guys, guys – "David said suddenly. "I heard it too!" Alessa shrieked. They glanced at Mia, who was kneeling down the passage. "The noise came from over there" she pointed inside. There was a roar and a scream again except louder.

"I think I know who it is – "Liam said, obviously trying not to smile. Then Alessa laughed. "Of course! It's Scaley!" she confirmed. "Oh, yeah!" David said. The four heads looked down the passage. "Who's Scaley?" Mia asked. "None of your business" David shot. "It's a Mammothian" Liam said. "What's that?" Mia asked curiously. "If you don't work with Brantley and come with us, you'll get to see him and know him" Alessa piped up. Mia's eyes immediately narrowed as she shook her head.

"Never, don't suggest that again" she said. "Oh, you can think that we'd listen to your ridiculous rules" David said marching to her. Before any of them could say anything, he gave Mia a rough punch on her head and she made some noise, stumbled backwards and fell down, unconscious. Liam went to Mia who was lying on the floor, and examined her. "Well, *someone*" he said, glaring at David "knocked her unconscious". David shrugged. "And we don't know if she's alive" Alessa added, also glaring at David.

"Of course she is!" David confirmed. "How do you know? Any proof?" Liam asked him. "Well, she's breathing" David replied. "Let me check" Alessa said, pushing the boys aside and marching to Mia. She fanned her hand near Mia's face and nodded. "She's definitely alive, probably knocked out" Alessa reported. "Good" Liam said. Then he frowned. "And bad" he added.

Smell the kitchen

"How do we wake her up?" David asked them. Liam thought for a while then said "How *can* we?" They tried to think of a way to wake her up. "A bucket of cold water?" Alessa suddenly suggested. "Great idea" David said "with a teensy weensy problem. Where do we get the water bucket?"

"Not very difficult to find that" Alessa said "Just sneak in the kitchen, fetch a decent sized bucked, fill cold water in it and bring it back". "And what if it doesn't work?" David asked. "Then we'll find another way of course" Alessa answered. "But that's a lot of work to do, sneak, find the bucket and water and all that" Liam said.

"If you two are going to sit and complain, alright, I'll go *myself*" Alessa said bossily. "Alright, alright, sorry, we'll come" Liam said. "Oh, great" Alessa said, her face brightened "So all we have to decide is who'll go and fetch the item without getting caught" Alessa explained. "I'll do it" Liam offered. "Probably you should" David and Alessa agreed. "All you need to do is that you find the kitchen, get a bucket, jug or whatever container you find – "Alessa instructed. "I know what to do; you both wait here, alright?" Liam said. "Yep" David said. Alessa nodded and said "Good luck".

So Liam snuck off and went down the stairs trying to smell the kitchen. He looked around the deserted hallway and ran hurriedly across it. He looked around and when he saw no kitchen, he ran back from where he came and suddenly caught the scent of apple pie. He sniffed deeply and tried to follow the scent which apparently led back upstairs.

He ended to a dining room where he saw Brantley and a few other important looking but armored men on the table, talking about some shady work. *The kitchen's got to be here somewhere,* he thought, looking around. Then he saw the kitchen. He galloped inside and saw the cook humming and stirring in the pot. *This isn't going to be easy,* he thought worriedly. Liam slipped inside and hid behind the stove. The cook changed her spot where she was standing and moved on to decorating the plum pie. Liam took a slow step.

Creak . . . he held his breath as the cook suddenly stopped humming. He saw her golden curls bobble as her pointy nose looked around and then she went on humming. He let out his breath in relief and went on searching. Then he spotted it.

A water jug! Filled with water! Here's my luck, he thought excitedly, grabbing the water jug and slipping quietly out of the kitchen. He ran and ran until he bumped on something.

Or was it someone?

She's dangerous

He looked up and saw an evil grinning face. "Caught ya sneakin', kid – "he barked when Liam, without thinking, threw the cold water in the jug on him and ran away. He rushed to the room and he saw David and Alessa seated back to back, looking bored. When they saw him come in, they smiled and said at once "Did you get it?" he nodded and held up the jug. They both jumped up. "Finally!" David yelled. "Give it to me, I'll throw it on her face" Alessa said, snatching the jug.

"Hang on" Liam said "We need a protection when she wakes up". David raised his brows. "What'd you mean?" he asked. "I mean, we can't be sure that she's still in the trance when she wakes up" Liam explained. "Good idea, Liam, but we have our disintegrators to protect us" David said. "Yeah, I know, I was just reminding you two to be prepared for anything she does; she's dangerous" Liam added.

So they rudely threw the water splash on her face and her eyes flew open at once. She gasped and looked around then trembled. "Brrr – where am I? Alessa!" Mia said as she got up. They explained what happened to her and Mia was very happy that Alessa thought of finding a way to wake her up. "Oh, Alessa!" she said, stepping forward to hug her but Alessa stepped back and pointed to her soaking wet shirt. "Better change before hugs" she advised her.

They didn't have any spare shirts for her, so she wasn't able to change her clothes. "I feel really cold and wet" Mia explained "And – um – sorry for twisting your hand, Dave, though honestly, I didn't know what I was doing, I tried to plan an escape, but it didn't work . . . ".

CHAPTER 7 – TO THE HIDEOUT

No waste of time

They climbed in the passage again and went deeper to find their way out; glad they had Mia and glad that David knocked her unconscious. "I *told* you" David was telling Liam "a little bump on her head would do the trick!" "Yeah, I thought it'd hurt" Liam replied. "It doesn't hurt, does it, Mia?" David asked her. "Not really, just a bit, but there *is* a bump, and it feels like it's probably as big as an orange" Mia answered, rubbing her bump. "Oh" David said, as he earned an *I'm-always-right* look from Liam.

They reached the top, and it was around four in the afternoon. "YOU ARE BACK!" a voice roared behind them. They turned and saw the Mammothian. Mia took some steps back, bumping on Alessa by mistake. "Oh no, oh no, oh no —"she said, backing off. "Shush!" Liam told her "He's a Mammothian, his name is Scaley". She looked up at Scaley, trying not to scream, but she believed one or two came out. Scaley grinned widely. "Scaley is the friendly Mammothian!" he bellowed, going closer to her.

Judging by the look on her face, David knew she didn't think he was. "It's okay" he said "we named him". Mia blinked. "What? But – how? He looks like he'll bite me!" she said. "Well, he won't, so don't scare yourself" David assured her "he doesn't know a thing! Except the fact that he's a Mammothian and that he can fight and that he knows who Brantley is" he added. Mia shrugged in reply.

"C'mon, you two" Liam dragged them with him "we can't waste another minute, could we?"

"We probably could if Mia didn't stop her drama of being a chicken in front of our team member –"Alessa said sternly. "Wait, wait, wait, wait – what do you mean *team member?* He's not - he's not our member, is he?" Mia stammered. "He is" Alessa said in a high and stern voice "and now *stop* freaking out just because of him and hurry up".

Helpless like a sheep

"She's right and no arguing *both* of you" Liam ordered. "OK, captain!" David said. Mia grinned and nodded. "Great! Let's go" Liam said. So they all decided to go to Brantley's hideout because they were sure that he'd be there with all his horrid servants.

They used the jet to ride back to their hideout. "Where'd you get this cool jet?" Mia asked when Liam offered her to try driving it after they all had turns. "We went to the jet shop and met Scaley there" Liam explained "Scaley *didn't* have a name, and he didn't even know what it was, so when we came up in the jet, we had loads of time. Then David told him about names, ages and all the other things, you know?" he asked. Mia nodded.

They taught her how to dive the jet and eventually reached the hideout. When they got down, they caught a figure running up to them. Alessa then shook Liam's sleeve. "Listen! I think its Sheepie!" she said, jerking her head on one side. They could hear her faint voice getting louder and louder "Oh, *there* you are! I can't tell you how worried I'd been about you! As soon as I saw dear little Mia taken away – are you alright, Mia? – Oh, no, I was *helpless* like- like- like a sheep! But then I remembered I *was* a sheep!" she shrieked hugging them tightly.

"Are you OK, Sheepie?" Mia asked, patting the sheep's wooly head. The sheep got on her back hooves and nodded. "How about you? And all of you? And – oh my, who's this?" she asked gazing steadily at Scaley as if he'd jump and bite her "Oh! I shouldn't've asked! It's a Mammothian!" Scaley smiled politely at the sheep and bowed. "Good day to you, ma'am" he tried to keep his voice in a decent tone.

"And with such nice manners! I'm good, lad, how about you?" she asked. "He's Scaley, Sheepie" Liam said "And, Scaley, this is Sheepie, that's her name, see?"

Apparently not

Soon, the six of them headed to the hideout and they carefully looked for an entrance. Suddenly, Mia's sharp eyes caught the door handle. "Guys! I think I found it!" she called to them. They all rushed to her and tried to push their way in and open the handle. "I'll do it now" Liam said, making his way through. He jiggled the handle, but nothing happened. "Let *me* try" David said, pushing Liam aside. He shook the handle hard and harder and the others started backing off to look for other places.

David furiously shook the doorknob. "David!" Liam said "be careful – "but it was too late. David had shaken the handle so hard that the door busted open. A loud bang echoed near the garden and all his friends gasped and crowded him. He turned and his face was, naturally, black due to the burst. "You weren't patient, were you?" Alessa asked, shaking her head. "Apparently not" David grinned. "Are you fine, though?" Liam asked. "I'm fine" he replied "and the door's opened!"

Liam peered in. A long dark hall welcomed them. "I wonder if anyone's here" he whispered. "The only way to find out is to go in" Sheepie said. So they marched in, looking around cautiously. "Only frames . . ." Mia said. "And lonely furniture's" Alessa added. "I think we're being watched" Liam said. They turned their heads around and shrugged. "I don't see anyone" David said. "We obviously can't see the person or spirit or bulgur or whatever . . ." Liam said in a low voice.

"Liam, you're scaring me" Mia said, tugging his sleeve when they began walking. "Sorry, but I *feel* like it –"Liam said. "Keep your feelings to yourself" David snapped. "Don't start now, David, you're getting annoying" Liam snapped back. "*Annoying? Do I need to tell you who are annoying? I will do it then! Or I'll show you!*" David roared. "Just – just shush" Liam said, trying to be polite. "He's right, David" Alessa said. David narrowed his eyes and looked away from Liam angrily. "Fine, do your things" he mumbled.

Murder and whisper

"Well, keep going" Mia said to Liam. He nodded and turned back to walking. Then they heard a cold voice "Fine day tomorrow and I'll make that Mia's funeral the saddest! She's still locked up with the other kids, so they'll work for me then I'll go back on my word". They gasped and saw Brantley and another man. The other man was wearing a high collar cape and a hat which was pulled down low, so they couldn't see his face. "Well, a good plan" the other man said in a deep voice "but I will kill the girl . . . can I not?" Brantley nodded. "You certainly can" he said.

The children's hearts were thumping so loud that they almost thought he'd hear it. They held their breath as Brantley got up and begun walking right and left continuously. "Then after she's dead, we'll get rid of the children and then we can capture that Kungawo trash and take the dimension to ourselves! What'd you think, Eduard?" he continued. "Sounds good, my friend" Eduard said "But to me, important is the murder, I have done plenty before, but never to a child. My daughter wasn't a child when she was . . . well, you know" he said "so how do I murder this Mia you talk about?"

Mia gripped Scaley and look of panic took over her face. Liam noticed and as good as a good leader, he put his hand on her shoulder and whispered "Its fine, we'll escape".

Then all his friends turned to him and stared at him in horror. "I'm serious" he said. They opened their mouths but no sound came out. He turned and looked behind him and jumped back when he saw Brantley's grinning face. "RUN!" he yelled, running. His friends shot off, but David grabbed his hand and ran with him. "Come back!" Brantley shouted, running after them. "You wish!" David shouted back.

But when they went out of the hideout, they saw the ghost soldiers. "They took my disintegrator!" Mia gasped, clutching at her belt where they stole it from. Then Brantley and Eduard, whoever he was, came out. Scaley growled and aimed his action. Sheepie waved her umbrella. Liam, Alessa and David pointed their guns. Mia held up her fists and positioned herself. "What's the best thing we can do to protect ourselves?" Mia asked from the corner of her mouth to David. "Run or team up and fight!" David replied. They looked at each other and agreed on the second one.

CHAPTER 8 – TEAM UP AND FIGHT

Let me go!

The battle began. Sheepie hit the stomachs of the Ghosts soldiers. Scaley was knocking them down nine by nine. Liam disintegrated whoever came in his way. Alessa used her best fighting skills that she learnt to use on her brother. David kicked hard on anyone. Mia punched on the jaws, ribs and stomach.

"What good is it to fight, you kids tell me?" Brantley said. "It's worth it" Alessa said, jumping out of a hammer crash that was meant to kill her. "It most certainly is not!" Eduard said. "No one asked you" David piped up, smashing one ghost soldier. Then Alessa screamed "LET ME GO!" and they all saw a Ghost soldier smash her on the floor.

"Alessa!" they shrieked. She was lifted up and smashed again and again. "Stop this!" Mia yelled. Liam tightened his hand on his disintegrator and fired it at the Ghost Soldier. The ghost soldier vanished and they hurried to her. "Is she awake?" Mia shook her. "I'm awake!" Alessa squeaked. "Are you fine?" Liam asked. "Yeah, yeah" she replied, getting up.

They – Liam, David, Mia, Alessa, Sheepie and Scaley – turned to Brantley who smiled coldly. "Well, we won this time, be back for another day, kids" he said, ushering his soldiers to follow him. They marched in the hideout and were gone. "Unfair!" Alessa said "just because I fell on the floor doesn't mean they won!" "Well, they won according to themselves" Liam told her.

No more lecture

"We have to attack again" Liam announced "and we need a spy to tell us what they're planning and we could track their location. That wouldn't be a problem, but the real problem is to be prepared for the fight. Disintegrator pistols aren't much help sometimes, you saw, didn't you? David, it was your pistol that Eduard snatched, wasn't it? You see?" his friends nodded "So we have to go back, put on some armor or something and prepare with our fists and kicks, alright?" Liam asked.

"Do we have to go to the weapon store?" Alessa asked. "I'm not sure . . ." Liam said, thinking. "I think we shouldn't go and fight Brantley at all. Maybe let's go back home" Mia said, suddenly scared. "That's not an option" Liam said, becoming severe and frowning. "Liam, you can't decide for us –"Mia began. "I can" Liam snapped "so don't start lecturing me". No more was said and they began to go back in the jet.

They drove it through the starry sky. "Are we nearly there?" Alessa asked. "We'll be by midnight" David replied; he was the one driving the jet. Then the jet shook. "Turbulence!" Mia screamed. "It's more than that!" Alessa yelled back "It's a crash!"

"STOP THIS THING!" Liam shouted.

"HOW – THE BREAKS ARE GONE!" David screamed.

"I NEVER THOUGHT I'D DIE SO SOON!" Alessa yelled.

"GOD, SAVE US!" Sheepie shrieked. Scaley roared. And they crashed.

The jet burst and all of them went flying in different directions, screaming. When the cloud of dust settled, there was a cough and Alessa's voice asked "Is everyone with us?" more coughs in response. "I'm here!" Sheepie called. "The Titanium Scaley is here, too" Scaley shouted. "I'm here, and David's with me" Mia yelled. But no answer from Liam.

Gold coins

When they got to each other, they looked around for him. "Look, there's a tower" David pointed at it. "Let's get inside" Sheepie said. So they all went in. Immediately, the lights went off, "What's happened?" Mia asked quickly. "I can't see anyone!" roared Scaley. "Oh no!" Alessa yelled. They all came back to back, but without realizing it. "Search for Liam!" David shouted. "In the dark?" Mia asked. "Yes!" he answered.

So they began to feel around and suddenly Mia gave a yell. "I think I felt him just now –"she screamed. "Ahem, it's me" Alessa informed her, yanking herself away. "Aw" Mia said, feeling other places. Suddenly, they heard weird rap music and disco lights began to flash.

"What in the world is this?" Alessa asked, barely able to see anyone or anything. "A dance stage?" David said, making a disgusted face, which his friends were unable to see unless the disco light flashed on him.

"I got him! I got him!" Scaley bellowed in his loud voice. "You didn't get him!" Sheepie squealed "You got me!" Scaley put her down and said "Sorry, ma'am!" Then the lights flickered on and the music died down. They all turned and blinked. "Oh – my – god" they gasped, staring. They saw an enormous hall with a lot gold coins. "These are stolen *gold coins!*" Alessa shrieked suddenly. "*Stolen?* Wow . . . "David said in a voice of wonder.

"Is this a dream, or real? Please tell me it's a dream" Mia said. "It is not" Alessa said "unless we're having the same dream"

"Oh, I hope we are" David added. "Where's Liam?" Scaley asked, the ground shaking. "We don't know" Mia replied. "Look! It's a wire!" Alessa pointed her finger to something lying on the floor. She picked it up and turned in over a few times. "That's not weird" David told her "it's normal to have wires around your room".

Math lessons, instead

"In *your* room it probably is" Alessa said "but not in normal people's rooms, unless it's a lab or something". "Well, whatever that wire is, it doesn't help us" Mia said, shrugging. "It probably does" said Alessa. They tried to find more things and they only found another wire. "I think I get it!" Alessa said, snatching the wires from them. She plucked the wires together and a bulb. Then the bulb glowed.

"It's the method to make it illuminate" Alessa explained "it's simple. Example you can call this wire A and this wire $B,$ all you have to do is join the wires, but that's the easy part. What's *most* important is that you know when you join the wires, nothing must explode. So to avoid the blast, we must make sure that the wires are not with any sort of liquid on it and the -"she was going to continue when Mia interrupted her. "I didn't really understand what you said . . ." she told her "But your explanation doesn't help us!"

"Alright" Alessa said, completely ignoring Mia's last part of her statement "I'll explain again. So, basically, the wires must have fallen off due to some wrong arrangement. The wires eventually began to fall –". "Alessa, we don't have much time for this" David said "you can give us your Math lesson –"

"Science!" Alessa interrupted.

"*Science lesson* later" David said. "I didn't understand anything, dear" Sheepie told Alessa. "It's alright, I'll explain it later" Alessa said. "Should we go in the hall?" Mia asked. "Probably" Sheepie answered. So they went in and looked around. It was very cold and they could hear raindrops outside. "It's- it's raining" Mia said. "Of course" David replied. After a while he turned to her and said, grinning "Are you scared?" Mia swallowed hard and shook her head.

"LIAM!" Scaley roared at one point. "Alessa" David said suddenly "Can't you use you math tech- I meant science techniques – to track Liam?"

"It won't work" Alessa replied "unless he wore a location tracker watch or something, which – with no doubt – he didn't"

Save the world

"Well, it's not very usual for people to wear location trackers – or whatever you call them – nowadays. Even before, I don't think they wore them" Mia said. "That's enough" David barged in "let's just keep quiet and look, more working less talking". So they continued searching: behind the curtains, under the table, behind the gold coins. But he wasn't anywhere.

"I'm sure he's doing something stupid!" David exclaimed, gritting his teeth. "Trying to save the world, I bet" Mia said. "Oh, dear" Sheepie said sadly. "Yeah" Alessa added "unless . . . of course! He's, well, stupid enough to go and look for some passage or anything he wants to find and he went off without us! It's really like him to not look for us and do something his way by himself!" she said worriedly. "So careless" David said. "But – it's impossible! He *must* be worried about us!" Mia cried out. "Well, it's not in him to be" Alessa told her "so forget it, let's make a plan"

"But he's our leader – Wait, what? Is he? Maybe" Mia protested. David gave her his well-known frustrated look. "Can you quit complaining, Mia?" he asked her, obviously trying not to yell angrily. "Arguing and complaining will not help!" Scaley yelled. "Alright, aright" Alessa said, covering her ears. "We searched *everywhere*" Mia yelled at David, who clenched his fists "This is *your fault!*"

"*My fault?*" he yelled back "Is it *my fault* because you don't have anyone else to blame?" Mia wrinkled her nose and shouted "No! It's your fault because *you* told us to search for Liam! *You* drove the jet! And *you* crashed it! So it's *all because of you!*"

"Oh, dear me!" Sheepie cried. "Stop!" Alessa said loudly "Stop yelling and blaming each other! Is that all you do, point fingers at each other?" Mia and David glared at each other, paying barely any attention to Alessa. "It's getting irritating" Alessa continued "and if you both *love* arguing, then all you need to do is to step right out of our team and let us know that your schedule is busy because you'll be arguing!"

I am the leader

"You're anything more than annoying, Alessa" David mumbled. Fortunately, Alessa didn't hear him. "So, listen up" she began, sitting down and curling her legs underneath her thighs "we're not going to look for Liam, but attack Brantley –"

"Are you sure if that's a good idea?" Scaley asked. "And, Alessa, we haven't won the last round" David explained "so, we can't expect to win this time". "We can, actually" Alessa interrupted. "Yes, my dears, we can!" Sheepie piped in. "We need Liam to guide us" Alessa reasoned. "I guess that's right . . ." Mia said. "That is *not* right" David said "Sometimes, we should do things without Liam and besides, didn't we agree that we'd not worry about him?" he asked.

"We did" Alessa replied. "So let's go back to Kungawo and tell him that Liam escaped from us" David told them. "Why don't you lead if you think that your so genius?" Mia asked. "I *am* leading" David said, as if it was the most obvious thing in the world. "Alright, go on, leader" Mia said, putting force on the last word. "Guys!" a voice screeched behind them. They saw Liam holding a box type of thing, but they didn't hesitate to hurry to him and yell questions in his ears.

"Liam! Where'd you go? We were so worried!" Mia shrieked.

"Where were you, Liam? Did you go away on purpose?" David shouted.

"Did you get lost? Were you even worried about us?" Alessa yelled at him.

"Oh, dear! Are you alright?" Sheepie asked.

"Scaley is happy to see Liam safe!" Scaley bellowed.

"Guys, relax!" Liam said to them "I'm fine! And I didn't go anywhere, I was just outside, looking for –"

"Us" David snapped. "No, looking for – "Liam said. "Us" Mia said. "No! I was looking for – "Liam said. "Us!" Alessa cried, narrowing her eyes. "NO!" Liam yelled at the top of his voice "I WAS SEARCHING FOR CLUES, NOT YOU!"

Talk to Kungawo

"Why exactly, I would like to know, were you searching for clues in the rain and not for us when we could be in more danger than the clues?" David asked in a dangerous, soft voice. "Well . . ." Liam said "Kungawo is in more danger than you guys". Alessa opened her mouth, very annoyed. "We could have been *killed* by god knows what might come and stab us!" she shrieked "And we could have caught a *cold* or freeze to *death* – don't you care? Kungawo is in his *castle!* It's safer than this unknown tower!" Liam was about to say something when David decided to barge in. "She's right! You can't just leave us like that! We were very worr-"he ranted. "*You* don't have to talk" Liam told him "I know how much worried *you* probably were way less than the number of slaps I'll give you!" When David heard this, he clutched his cheek and narrowed his eyes. "OK" Mia mumbled "Can you just tell us what you're holding?" Liam glared at David and said "I would have told it earlier is *someone* didn't try to lecture me!" he said, still glaring at David, who slouched.

"Alright, enough with that, just tell us what that box is" Alessa said. "Well, it's not *really* a box" Liam began, starting to soften his voice "It's actually a communication device directly to Kungawo". "But- when did he give it to you?" Mia asked. Liam smiled. "Long before you knew" he said, stepping back. That's when they noticed that he was wearing an armor kind of thing.

"WOW" they exclaimed. "Where did you get that?" Alessa asked. "Have you been in invisible meetings?" Mia joked. "Nothing that mysterious" Liam laughed "It's all from Kungawo" he added, shrugging. David gritted his teeth, feeling a bit jealous. "But, why didn't he give it to us? And when did he give it to you?" He asked.

"Not very long ago, and he gave it to me because it was supposed to be for me" Liam said. They boys exchanged small smiles. The others grinned. "They're getting along, thank god" Mia whispered. Alessa tried not to laugh because Mia argued more than Liam did. But the master of arguing was David.

Go jet gone

"Let's go to Kungawo and ask him to give *us* armor like that!" David told them. "Yeah, he'll probably give you guys, along with some cool weapons" Liam said. "What weapon do *you* have?" Mia asked. "Oh, a disintegrator pistol" Liam replied. "Great! Let's go!" Alessa exclaimed. "Wait, we don't have our jet" Liam began, glancing at David, who was the driver and lost control of the gears.

"I can fly, remember?" Scaley said. They hadn't remembered so they mounted on his back and they flew. "Wow!" David yelled, as the wind seemed to be slower than them. Liam, who was obviously sitting in the front, shouted "There's the castle! Scaley, land!" So Scaley landed with a thump in front of the castle.

CHAPTER 9 – ARMOR AND FIGHT

Yikes!

Sakura opened the castle door. "I expected to see you" she said. "Oh, what – is that a Mammothian?" she asked, backing off. "Don't worry, it's friendly, I was scared of it at first, too" Mia informed her. "Oh, I suppose your right, well, Mammothian's don't have names" Sakura said. "We figured that much out when we met him" Liam told her. "We're here because we sort of lost the battle, but we'd be good and up for a round two if Kungawo gives us the armor like Liam!" David said. "Alright, well, come inside! But mind you, the Mammothian shouldn't knock a thing over!" Sakura said, gesturing them to come inside the castle.

They heard the loud rumble of the thunder and the lights flickered then went off. "Yikes!" Mia screamed, right next to David's ears. He gave her a hard shove, not knowing he gave *her* the shove. "Oww!" Mia yelled. "Oh, dear, me!" Sheepie exclaimed. A dim fire torch silenced them. "Shh!" Sakura scolded them "You're making a racket". "Mia is" David said, covering his ear where she had yelled. "Sorry, I didn't know" Mia said "and besides, it's completely your fault

56

that you stood next to *me*". David opened his mouth to say something when Sakura pushed Mia and David in a room and locked it.

"You both will stay there and argue till the mission is over" she called. "How dare you!" David's furious voice said. "I dare to" Sakura replied, making the others laugh. "You and Mia can stay there and yell as loud as possible" Liam said, laughing. He could hear them growling at each other. They went to the hall and Kungawo was seated on a table, talking to some unknown people. "Kungawo!" Alessa and Liam yelled. Kungawo removed his glasses and said "The Mammothian must stay out" So Scaley sulkily went out.

"What is wrong?" Kungawo asked. They explained everything to him. It took about fifteen minutes to tell him and he asked them to repeat it. So they had some food and told him. "And we need the armor to defend ourselves!" Alessa pleaded. "Yes, noble Kungawo!" Sheepie added. "Alright, where are David and Mia? Fetch them!" he ordered getting up. Liam and Sheepie went to the room where they both were locked. Liam unlocked it and saw them both fighting. David was pulling Mia's hair and she was punching him hard on his jaw.

Fight without armor

"This is what happens when you lock us in a room!" David said. "Well, you both are fighting" Liam said "Like any other day" he shrugged. "Grr!" Mia growled at David, pulling her back, and marching to Liam. "Well, did you ask him?" she asked as they all began walking back to the hall. "Yep" Liam replied "he's probably going to give it to you in a while! There are weapons with it. The armor, I mean".

The children excitedly made their way to Kungawo's hall. "Well, bruises, steam pouring out of your ears, glaring and growling . . . all I can guess you both have been fighting!" Kungawo told Mia and David. "They have" Sheepie confirmed. "I assumed" Alessa said.

"Anyway, the armor, Kungawo?" David said "Oh and Liam said that they have weapons". "They do" Kungawo said. He then called Sakura and asked "Will you please fetch the armor suits I prepared?" "Of course, sir" she replied and went. "You knew we'd need armor?" Alessa asked. "I did" Kungawo answered. "How?" David asked. "Because you can't fight without armor" Kungawo answered. "I *can!*" David yelled "Mia and I have fought without armor!" "Yes, you know very well I do not mean it *literally*" Kungawo scolded him. Sakura reappeared minutes later. "For David, for Mia and for Alessa" she handed him the armor. Kungawo turned to the children, who were anxiously watching him.

"This is for you, David" he said, giving him the armor. David eagerly took it and examined it. "This is for Alessa" Kungawo said, handing Alessa her armor over. "And finally, Mia!" he gave Mia her armor. They were taken to the changing rooms and they came out and admired their armors. "I look so fierce!" Mia said, turning over her cape and adjusting her high collar. Alessa straightened her skirt. David patted his chest armor. "Well!" Sakura said, smiling at them "You all look like warriors!" They laughed and walked to the hall, boasting about their armors. "Mine is so cool yet comfortable!" Alessa bragged. "My armor makes me look very fierce" Mia boasted. "Well, mine is better than *any* of you both!" David said. Sakura led the way, the kids arguing. Kungawo and Liam were waiting in the hall.

User guide

Liam's eyes widened when he saw their armors. "Wow! You guys look great!" he said. "I know!" David said making sure that everyone saw his clawed glove. "Thanks!" Alessa said. "That's what I thought!" Mia said, grinning. "Well, now I will hand you the weapons, alright?" Kungawo said. They nodded excitedly.

He gave David first: a long, thick rope. Then Mia got a spear and Alessa was given a long shiny silver sword. "Do you like them?" Kungawo asked. He smiled at the children admiring their weapons. "Of course yes!" David said. "I wish I knew how to use this" Mia said, waving the spear in the air like a wand. "Stop!" Alessa cried "That's *certainly* not how you use it". Mia thought for a second. Then she tried to spin the spear. "Is – is it working, Mia?" David called. "Doesn't look like it is!" Mia called back. "It's more like she'd rip the curtains apart if she keeps going" Liam muttered to David. "Stop it, Mia!" Alessa said. So Mia took a halt.

"*How* to use this thing?" Mia asked Kungawo. "I will show you" Kungawo told her, getting up and taking the spear from her hand. The Team and Sakura took a side, as Kungawo began to fight with a make believe enemy. It looked quite odd, but they understood the example. "You see, and you should protect like that, poke like that – only in the stomach or ribs, though – and use the back of the spear to spank his middle" he explained while doing the actions.

"Wow!" Mia said, amazed to have such a cool weapon. "I *like* that!" She took the spear from Kungawo. "Can you – can you *teach* me?" Mia asked. "Of course I can, but, do you know, spear is an easy weapon" Kungawo explained "and a clever kid like you would learn it pretty fast" he patted her head. Mia pouted, confused. "But, just what Liam said, I'd tear a curtain to make use of it" she said, looking up to him. "No, no, it's not for that purpose" Kungawo insisted. "But what if I *don't* know how to use it?" Mia asked worriedly. "You'll figure it out in a matter of time, Mia; don't worry about those silly things" Kungawo told her. Mia shrugged and went to Alessa.

"Any idea how you're going to use *that?*" she hissed in her ear. "Sword. . . "Alessa murmured "no idea". "C'mon then, I will show you" Kungawo suggested. He began to fight with an imaginary person and picked up the moves. When Kungawo gave the sword back to her so she could show him what she understood, it looked like she didn't need any swords lessons. "This is meant to be mine!" she said happily. Her friends grinned at her. "It's my turn!" David said, hopping to Kungawo.

Rename it

Kungawo showed him how to snatch things with the ropes and fight with it, but when his turn came, he only got tangled in the ropes. "How . . . to . . . use . . . this?" David panted. The children laughed and untangled him, and then Kungawo did every step slowly and clearly. It was a long time when David got the hang of it. "I'm doing it! I'm really doing it!" he yelled "It's like dance- fighting!" He was sort of swaying with the ropes, but it looked weird.

"You're all great at it" Liam told his friends. "Thanks" Alessa said, shining her sword.

"I look so awesome when I use my ropes! Actually, I think I'll call them lizard tails . . . or perhaps snake tongue . . . "David said. Alessa gave a shriek. "Ahh! Don't call it that! Maybe just keep the name ropes!" she screamed.

While David and Alessa argued about the name, Mia didn't look too happy. "What's up?" Liam asked her. She made a tired face then laughed. "I have no idea how to use this spear! It's a bit hard" she sighed. "Maybe you should practice" Liam said, smiling a bit. Mia raised her eyebrows. "Probably" she said, sighed again, a bit more dramatically. Then they heard David's loud suggestions for the name and Alessa's piercing shrieks.

"I'm naming it fish liver!" David's voice said.

"Yikes, no! Don't do that! Name it apple or something!" Alessa shrieked.

"I'm sticking to name it Fish liver!"

"No!"

Liam grinned and turned to his friends. They both were shooting dagger- eyes and scowling at each other. "Stop, you two" Liam laughed. "Well, if he calls that rope fish liver or jellyfish boogies – they don't have boogies – it's gross!" Alessa said. "I am *not* calling it jellyfish boogie, alright?" David shot back. "Who cares what you call it?" Mia barged in. "Uh oh, don't let this be an epic fight" Liam muttered. The other three were yelling at each other.

"Who asked *you* to join, Miss Wormy Pants?" David asked irritatingly.

"Shut up! And Miss Wormy Pants is *better* than Mister Wormy Underpants! And that's you!" Mia growled angrily.

"How dare you!" David growled back.

"Shush it, you both!" Alessa shouted.

Liam slapped his forehead and said "Oh my god, when'll you finish?" the children frowned at each other and then at Liam. "Now if they stop" David grunted. "I'll stop when *he* stops" Mia thundered. "I'll stop now, then" Alessa said, shrugging and earning a grateful smile from Liam. "Well, I should thank you" Liam said, sighing. "You should thank me, *after* they thank you, for shushing me, so thank you" Alessa said "but thank me after they don't yell thanks in *your* ears-"

Scared, no offense

"Thanks" Liam interrupted her. "Thanks" Mia said. "Thanks" David said, his voice rising. "Thanks!" Mia yelled at David. "OK, you should stop" Liam told them. "Shush!" Alessa said. "Thanks" Liam replied. "Alright, children" Kungawo said, snapping then back to business. "Now you will attack Brantley and Eduard. You need to leave. Now! And your jet is fixed, my assistant got it. It is outside. Go, now! Good luck!" he said.

Before the children left, Sakura hugged them. "Goodbye, nice children" she half sobbed "I hope you all will return alive". The children shuddered. "What'd you mean come back alive? Of course we'll be alive!" David snapped.

They went on the jet and shot off in the night. "So dark . . ."Alessa whispered in a voice that made the others shiver. "Stop that!" Sheepie said. They zoomed like a rocket, with Scaley roaring at the top of his lungs. The raindrops splattered on the jet roof, sounding like people were throwing little heavy balls at the jet. Mia smiled at Alessa and gripped her arm. "I'm scared, Alessa" she whispered. "But why are you smiling then?" Alessa whispered back. "Because a smile would make me feel less scared, and besides I'm not the only one scared here" Mia replied, with quite an offense taken. "I didn't mean- I didn't mean any offense" Alessa assured her.

Mia shrugged and pointed at David with her mouth. Liam was driving the jet this time. David was talking to Sheepie at the back of the jet. Scaley was peering out of the window, grinning widely. "Are you ready, guys?" Liam asked, glancing over his shoulder to look at his friends. "Yes!" Mia said at once. Liam grinned, remembering that Mia didn't want to fight Brantley in the beginning. "Yep!" Alessa and Sheepie said, smiling at one another. "You bet!" Scaley yelled. "Yeah, I was born for this task!" David said. "I guess we're set then" Liam told them "We have to be quick, not scared and we shouldn't start giving insults to each other in the middle of the fight or start running around, while yelling some math - science- lessons" he added. They all laughed and went on with talking.

"We haven't eaten in a long time" Mia informed them. "We didn't" Alessa agreed. Then she looked a bit thoughtful. "I wonder when we'll reach the castle" she said. "Nothing to worry about!" David said "We'll be there in no time!" He marched to Liam, whose eyes were focused on the sky and the road below. "Let me drive, Liam, please move" he said. Liam turned and shook his head. "We can't risk crashing the jet again, David, you could drive on our way back" he explained. David groaned and went back to Sheepie. "Who made him leader?" he grumbled to Sheepie. Sheepie smiled when Liam said loudly "I am not the leader, in fact, you can take the gears if you want now".

Fake sob

David's blue eyes brightened but he was still confused why Liam. He got up and grabbed the gears and went on top speed. "What's up? Anyone home?" he asked, knocking lightly on Liam's head. Liam grinned and said "No one's home". "We're here!" Alessa squealed. So they were. The jet landed, but . . .

CRASH! Yelps and shouts were heard. "The jet crashed!" Mia wailed. "It's your fault!" Alessa said, pointing at David. "No! It's Liam's fault" David said. "What? How?" Liam protested. "You allowed me to drive the jet!" David told him. Scaley then roared with all his might, it seemed. "Mean Brantley's castle is over there!" he shouted. "Yes, let's go" Liam said, getting up and brushing the dust off his armor. "Oh, dear!" Sheepie cried.

They slowly and quietly, and one could sense the cold and uncomfortable silence in the air. Liam, after taking a deep breath, said "We have to be careful, Team, we can't let those twerps win this time, do your best". Mia gave a small sniff. David made a slightly concerned face. Alessa looked as if someone fed her a live slug. Sheepie gasped and Scaley gave a fake sob. "Alright?" Liam asked a bit scared himself. "Right" Mia said.

They all marched to the castle, feeling quite nervous. They had weapons, but they still didn't feel safe, though the thought that they all were together did calm them a little. "Scaly and David" Liam began "You both will be partnered up. Alessa and Sheepie can also be a pair. That leaves me and Mia, we both can partner, alright?" he said. "Yes" Mia answered. The rest of them nodded. "I could make you and David" Liam told Mia "But you both'll start arguing silly, and especially with

Brantley standing right there, ready to kill us, it's not a very good idea to fight against each other" he added. Ten lectures later, they stood near the fence of the castle.

"Well!" David said. "Well?" Mia asked nervously. "Open the gates" Liam said, stepping forward and pushing the gates open. Immediately, Ghost Soldiers appeared and charged at the team. And the battle began.

Sweet little girl

David started on one group of them standing stupidly, and he first punched them all to make them dizzy, and then he tripped them on his ropes and beat them up. Liam found his weapon easy and he just disintegrated all of the soldiers. Alessa sliced them in halves with her sword, realizing that ghosts can't be harmed with blades. But it didn't matter to her; she did her job slicing them like carrots. Mia had a bit of difficulties, but she understood the tricky parts. Scaley used claws, though the look of him frightened a big number of the Ghost Soldiers. Sheepie swung her umbrella wildly. Then the castle door burst open.

The battle paused and they stared at the three figures that marched out. The one in the middle wore a long cape-gown sort of thing and had a very familiar smirk. It was Brantley. The one on his left wore a dark hat to cover his face and he had a high collar coat. The one on his right was completely unfamiliar, but it was a girl. She had shiny black hair and a cape-gown like Brantley. But her face wasn't wearing a look of smirk, it was smiling evilly. She looked worse than Brantley. "Who *is* that?" asked Mia; she was staring at the strongly built girl with her mouth wide open.

"Whoever she is, it doesn't matter to us" David said, and he resumed to the battle. "Well, she might" the girl said. She had a rough but flat voice and to anyone, she'd sound like a sweet little girl of fourteen, but definitely not look like one. "Oh, you sound so . . . weird" Sheepie stated. The girl snorted and took a quick step forward and before Sheepie knew it, she punched the sheep on her stomach so she went flying and screaming. "Sheepie!" Alessa screamed. She hurriedly turned back to the Ghost Soldier who was charging at her. David glared at the girl then his eyes darted to the unknown, mysterious man standing stiffly next to Brantley, who was still smirking.

"Stay away from that girl!" Liam yelled to Mia, who had taken some angry steps to her "She can be dangerous!" Mia stopped. She turned to Liam who was holding a Ghost Soldier helmet. "Look, we are in a battle, it *is* dangerous" Mia told him sternly. After a moment, Liam nodded to her. "Alright, you could fight her then. But be careful!" he called as Mia continued storming to the girl, who leapt to action. "Oh, hello, little squirrel" the girl said, smiling infuriatingly. Mia gritted her teeth, not able to think of anything to say. "I am *not* a squirrel, you sausage" she said, thinking of something harsh to say and coming up with sausage at the end. The girl laughed dauntingly. "Me? A sausage? Very funny" she said, still laughing, which annoyed Mia very much.

You work for me

She strode up to her and growled like a tiger. She picked up her spear and aimed it at the girl, who hopped away, out of her sight. "Ohh! The squirrel has some powers, I see" she said, kicking Mia on her shins. "Oww!" Mia cried, gripping her shins. "No time for this, little squirrel" the girl said, waving a sword in the air "Didn't anyone tell you that girls like you can't fight properly? You look like a – whoa!" she dodged a punch. "You talk too much" Mia grumbled. Then she took the other end of her spear and – remembering Kungawo's example- she dug it hard in the girl's ribs. The girl gave a gasp and clasped her ribs.

Mia felt a hand on her shoulder and she turned to see David grinning. "She's exaggerating" Alessa said from behind him. "That was super cool, Mia!" She exclaimed. Mia rolled her eyes and laughed. "Thanks" she replied. "Stop celebrating!" Liam shouted from the other side "we're not done yet!" they turned back to the girl who was already gone.

Brantley marched up to Liam and before Liam could disintegrate him, he snatched up the gun and threw it over his shoulder. Liam opened his mouth to scream 'unfair' but it seemed to be too late. Brantley grinned and said "It's over, Liam. Now you work for me, or die".

"I am *not* working for you!" Liam said, not knowing why he suddenly didn't feel scared. He heard a yelp and turned to look at Alessa being thrown from the other side to his side. When Alessa halfway, he saw her eyes widen. "Liam! Look out!" she yelled and threw her sword at Brantley. He was just in time to flip on the other side because Brantley had flung his own sword at Liam and he was thrown back because Alessa had shot her sword at him. It wasn't a very good aim since Brantley didn't die, but it was enough time for Liam to fetch Alessa's sword and run away from Brantley. Ghost Soldiers were scattering around and the man who had come with Brantley was still standing where he was before. Liam found him very creepy. He was standing in the same position, his head cocked on one side like it was before and he was standing on the exact right spot.

Graceful leap of burp

He spotted Alessa scurrying back from where she fell. And he also noticed her spectacles were crashed. "We'll get new ones" he told her. She blinked. "New ones? What?" she asked. "Oh, sorry" Liam said "I meant new spectacles". She grinned and nodded and went off to deal with the Ghost Soldiers.

David was having an excellent time. He didn't have any trouble at all tangling the Ghost Soldiers. He even spanked them with his ropes. He also found it very easy to dodge rope type of things like thin tree branches and thin arms and thin feet and thin things that came in his way.

Alessa didn't have a weapon because Liam had hers and he needed it. She knew she couldn't fight without her sword, so she kicked a Ghost Soldier and snatched his sword instead.

The fighting lasted for a long time and the creatures that passed by the castle joined in to help whoever side they were on. Liam realized it was time to end the battle so he gave Brantley a hard shove that made him stumble to someone who he really didn't want to. Scaley burped loudly and he immediately went flying to Alessa, who swung her sword and then he crashed on Mia's feet and she stomped her spear on him and with a graceful leap, David tangled him. He and Mia finally threw him to Scaley again and Scaley sent him flying towards the sun rising. The Ghost Soldiers dropped their weapons and they rushed towards the sunrise, as if they would catch Brantley. The mysterious man made a move at last and went back in the castle.

The team looked at each other happily. "We did it, didn't we?" David said at last. "We did!" Mia yelled excitedly as she squeezed Alessa's and David's arms. "That was *awesome!*" Alessa cried, hugging everyone. "It was . . . but . . ." Liam said slowly. "But what?" Mia asked, after she was done leaving bruises on Alessa's arm. "We need to get Sheepie" he said, hating to destroy the celebration. There was a stunned pause. "Well, what are we waiting for?" David asked, positioning to action "Let's *go!*" And off they went to fetch her.

The team Jetsine

"I think she went that way" Mia said as they ran as quietly as possible because they tried not to wake anyone. They followed her as she made her way quickly to the deserted building. When they finally saw the building, they stopped. "She's got to be here somewhere" Mia said. "Hmm" Alessa said "From which way did she fall?" she asked Mia. Mia pointed from the rising sun till the side that was still dim of the city. "Then" Alessa said "She should possibly be there!" she pointed to a bunch of trash cans. David laughed. "Trash cans? How do you-"he said when they heard a moan from the trash cans. "She *is* here!" Liam said, removing the piles of trash to rescue her out. "She – well- didn't seem to bother crawling out of there earlier, though" Mia said, making her confused face.

All of them agreed to this, but they knew they could expect that from Sheepie. They went back to the castle and saw their jet. "Strange! Wasn't it broken?" David asked, leaping inside followed by the others. "Yeah, is this even our jet?" Mia asked. "It is" a female voice said, making the jet shake. "Who said that?" Liam asked, suddenly scared. "I am a talking jet, and I have been spying on you folks for a long time" the jet said "I am Jetsine and . . . well, that's it". Liam was astounded.

But he said "Well, welcome to our team, Jetsine!" and everyone smiled, trying not to laugh because it looked silly that they were smiling at nothing. The jet went off, back to Kungawo's castle. They didn't even have to knock on the door because Sakura opened it at once and pulled them in. "My dears!" she cried. They calmed her and she took them to Kungawo, who was smiling. "I am very happy and proud of you all!" Kungawo said, beaming at them. They all smiled in pleasure. "Thank you, Kungawo, for giving us the armors, weapons and encouragement" Liam said, grinning at his friends.

"And thank *you* for letting me get my powers back" Kungawo said as he hugged them "All of you did a good job!" Sheepie beamed and Scaley roared happily and the children just hugged Kungawo back. They all went out, including Sakura who wanted to hear the whole story. They told them about Jetsine, too, who was parked in front of the castle. She politely went front and back in greeting. In the end of the story, Sakura insisted that they all deserved some tea, much to Alessa's excitement and she was careful to blow her tea before drinking it.

Times up!

Few minutes later, it was time for them to get back to the real world. Before they left, Kungawo gave them some accessories that was related to The Invisible Dimension. He gave Alessa a better necklace that opened the portal to The Dimension, he gave Liam a watch that he could use to communicate with them, he gave Mia a bracelet that she could use it to control things and David got shades so he could see the creatures that are invisible in the normal world. They thanked him and said goodbye. And in the portal they went.

They fell outside, next to the enchanted rock and they found themselves wearing their own clothes, not the armors. "Wow! I feel home again!" David said, making the others laugh. "Home? Couldn't you feel it before, too? Weird!" Mia said. They went back to Mia's house and there stood Mia's parents, Alessa's mother, David's Father and Liam's grandmother. "Where have you been?" Mia's mother shrieked. "Nowhere" David said "don't be worried! Dad, I got shades but- hey! You can't have them!" he snatched back his shades. "We went for a camp outside" Liam lied, trying not to worry them "and you and Elena were asleep so we decided to tell you later when we came back. But we changed our mind and stayed for . . . uh, three days . . . was it?" he asked Alessa. She shrugged.

"Well, we *have* been extremely worried, but at least you're alright" Liam's grandmother said as she hugged him. All the families said farewell and headed to their homes. Then the children waited patiently for the next mission to call them.

End

About the Author

Best known as the home made author of several unpublished books of all time— Zara Hassan has challenged and changed the way tens of millions of kids around the world think about fiction and fantasy. She is an entrepreneur, educator, and story teller who believes the world needs more education, class and elegance to help flourish a harmonized society.

With perspectives on fact and fiction that often contradict conventional wisdom, Zara has earned a reputation for straight talk, irreverence, and courage and has become a passionate and outspoken advocate for education.

Zara Hassan is founder of "little friend" strawberry flavored lip balm which is halal, organic and handmade.

Zara has been heralded as a visionary who has a gift for simplifying complex concepts—ideas related to society, life hacks, social justice, and economics—and has shared her personal journey in her upcoming personal journal in ways that resonate with audiences of all ages and backgrounds.

Her core principles and messages—like "teach them how to fish, don't buy them fish".

Her writings encourage people to become educated and help others take an active role in education.

To learn more, write to <u>curious.zara145</u> with Gmail domain.